Meet Ezra.

Ezra is fourteen years old.

He lives on the planet Lothal.

Ezra lives in an empty tower

outside the city.

He lives alone,

but that is fine with Ezra.

Ezra is good at living alone.
He knows how to take care
of himself.

Lothal is under control of the Empire.

Ezra doesn't like the Empire.

He thinks the people of Lothal

should be free.

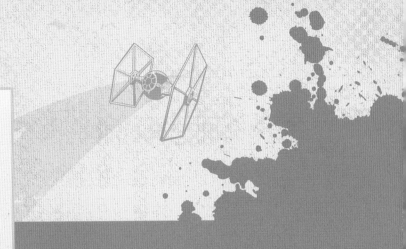

One day Ezra was out walking.
He heard a loud sound and
looked up.

He saw a TIE fighter

chasing a starship through the sky.

The TIE fighter was from the Empire.

The starship fired at the TIE fighter.

The TIE fighter fell out of the sky and crashed not far away.

Ezra didn't like the TIE fighter.

Ezra ran to the crashed TIE fighter.

He pounded on the window of the ship.

Ezra climbed onto the ship

and tried to pull open the hatch.

It was stuck.

The pilot couldn't get out.

Ezra pulled and pulled

until the hatch opened!

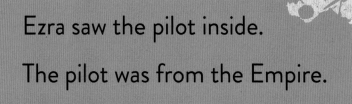

Ezra saw the pilot inside.

The pilot was from the Empire.

He was very angry.

He told Ezra to get off his ship.

The pilot did not even say
thank you to Ezra for helping him.
Ezra thought that was rude.

The pilot did not want Ezra's help.

He thought he was better

than Ezra.

Ezra had a plan.

He would teach the pilot a lesson.

Ezra decided to take parts

from the broken ship.

Ezra reached behind the pilot.

He took a gadget from the ship.

The pilot didn't see.

Then Ezra grabbed the pilot's helmet
and jumped off the ship!

The pilot realised what Ezra had done and became even angrier.

He turned on the ship's cannons!

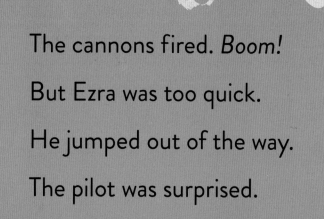

The cannons fired. *Boom!*

But Ezra was too quick.

He jumped out of the way.

The pilot was surprised.

Ezra took out his special slingshot.

He fired it at the TIE fighter.

Ezra's shot bounced off the ship
and hit the pilot in the head!
The pilot was knocked out!

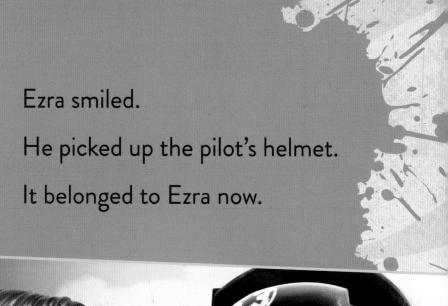

Ezra smiled.

He picked up the pilot's helmet.

It belonged to Ezra now.